Dirty Bertie

FLEAS!

For Jane, for all your scootering across
London on your moped to collect
and deliver *Bertie* bits and pieces.
A big thank you ~ D R

For Laurie, who's not as dirty as he'd
like to be ~ A M

STRIPES PUBLISHING
An imprint of Little Tiger Press
1 The Coda Centre, 189 Munster Road,
London SW6 6AW

A paperback original
First published in Great Britain in 2006

Characters created by David Roberts
Text copyright © Alan MacDonald, 2006
Illustrations copyright © David Roberts, 2006

ISBN: 978-1-84715-005-9

The right of Alan MacDonald and David Roberts to
be identified as the author and illustrator of this work
respectively has been asserted by them in accordance
with the Copyright, Designs and Patents Act, 1988.

Printed and bound in China.
STP/1000/0029/1012

10

Dirty Bertie

FLEAS!

DAVID ROBERTS WRITTEN BY ALAN MACDONALD

Stripes

Contents

CHAPTER 1

SCRATCH! SCRATCH! SCRATCH!

Bertie was reading his comic at the table.

"Bertie, do you have to do that?"
asked Mum.

"What?"

"Keep scratching like that. You're
worse than a dog."

"I can't help it, I'm itchy," said Bertie.

Dirty Bertie

He went back to his comic.

Scratch! Scratch! He scratched his leg under the table. Scratch! Scratch! He scratched under his pyjama top. Scratch! Scratch! He itched his arm.

"BERTIE! What's wrong with you?" said Mum.

"Sorry," shrugged Bertie. "I'm itchy all over."

"Let me take a look at you," said Mum. She rolled up his sleeve to inspect his arm. A look of horror appeared on her face. "Oh no! Fleas!"

"FLEAS?" cried Suzy.

"FLEAS?" cried Dad.

"Where? I can't see them!" said Bertie, peering at his arm curiously. Mum pointed at the tiny red dots above his elbow.

"There," she said. "Those are flea bites."

Suzy shifted her chair away from
Bertie. "Ugh! Keep away! I don't want
your fleas."

She scratched her hair. Maybe her
grubby little brother had given her fleas
already. Maybe she had flea bites all over
her! She fled from the table and dashed
upstairs to the bathroom.

"But where did he get them?" asked
Dad.

"I bet I can guess," said Mum, grimly.

Dirty Bertie

Whiffer was in the lounge, dozing peacefully in an armchair. Scratch! Scratch! Scratch! His back leg swished like a windscreen wiper.

"There!" said Mum. "Just as I thought. There's the fleabag."

Bertie bent over to take a closer look. It was true. Whiffer's fur was alive with tiny black creatures hopping around like … well, like fleas.

Dirty Bertie

"Good grief!" said Mum. "He's crawling with them!"

"Wow! Millions!" said Bertie.

"Enough to start a flea circus," muttered Dad, keeping his distance.

"What's a flea circus?" asked Bertie.

"Oh you used to get them years ago," said Dad. "Performing fleas – doing tricks and things."

Bertie could hardly believe his ears. A flea circus! With performing fleas! What a fantastic idea! He'd already tried to train his pet earthworm, but Mum had put a stop to that when she found Arthur in his bed. But fleas? That was a much better idea. Fleas could jump and hop so surely they could be trained to do other things? Like acrobatics. Fleas turning somersaults.

Fleas standing on each other's shoulders. Fleas flying through the air on a flea trapeze! All he had to do was catch some of Whiffer's fleas and he could have his very own circus.

Dirty Bertie

Mum had Whiffer by the collar and was pulling him out of the armchair.

"We've got to do something," she said. "Fleas spread. They lay their eggs everywhere. They're probably all over the furniture by now!"

Just thinking about it made Dad feel itchy. "How do you get rid of them?" he asked.

Mum dragged Whiffer through the kitchen and out of the back door.

"You can buy flea shampoo — but someone will have to bath him."

"I'll do it!" said Bertie.

"NO!" said both his parents at once.

"He'll have to go to the vets," said Mum, eyeing Dad. "You can take him."

"Why me?" said Dad. "I took him last time!"

Dad remembered their last visit all too well. The vet had tried to force a pill down Whiffer's throat. Whiffer had spat it out three times.

"Well I can't do it," said Mum flatly. "I'm taking Suzy shopping this morning."

"But I've got work to do!" protested Dad.

"This is an emergency," said Mum. "The house is crawling with fleas. Bertie's already been bitten. They won't just walk out of the door, you know."

"All right, all right," groaned Dad. "I'll take him."

CHAPTER 2

Bertie waited till Mum and Suzy had gone out. He crept out of the back door, armed with his flea collecting kit. Whiffer wagged his tail, pleased to see him.

Bertie crouched beside him with a toothbrush and a matchbox. With a little coaxing he managed to get a few of the fleas on the end of the toothbrush.

Dirty Bertie

He shook them into the matchbox
and slid the lid shut quickly.

"BERTIE!" called Dad from indoors.
"Can you come here a minute?"

Bertie stuffed the matchbox into his
pocket and went inside.

Dad was working at the computer in
the back room.

"Bertie," he said. "Are you busy right
now?"

"Not especially," said Bertie.

"I was thinking. Maybe you'd like to

take Whiffer to the vets? He's your dog."

"No thanks. Can I go now?"

"Wait!" said Dad, desperately. "I'll pay you."

Bertie paused in the doorway. "How much?"

"Two pounds."

Bertie thought about it. As usual he'd spent all his pocket money.

"Three," said Dad. "Okay, five pounds – that's my last offer."

"Done!" said Bertie. He held out his hand.

"Oh no," said Dad. "You don't get paid until the job's done. And you'd better ask Gran to go with you."

Bertie nodded. Five pounds – he could do a lot with that. He was already planning what he needed for his flea circus.

Dirty Bertie

DING DONG! Bertie rang Gran's doorbell.

"Hello, Bertie!" said Gran, opening the door. "What a nice surprise. Come in!"

"I better not," said Bertie. "Dad wants me to take Whiffer to the V-E-T-S."

"The what?" said Gran.

Bertie lowered his voice. "The vets."

"Oh, the VETS! Why are you whispering?"

"Because I don't want Whiffer to hear. He hates the vets."

Gran looked behind him. "Who's going with you?" she asked.

"Ah," said Bertie. "Well…"

"I see," said Gran. "I'd better get my coat then."

"So what's the matter with Whiffer?"
asked Gran, as they headed up the road
with Whiffer on his lead.

"Oh, nothing much. He's just got fleas."

"FLEAS?" Gran stopped dead.

"Yes," said Bertie. "Loads of them!
You should take a look, Gran – it's like a
flea party!"

Dirty Bertie

"No thanks," said Gran. "I'll take your word for it." She shook her head. "No wonder your dad didn't want to come. Typical! 'Ask your gran. She'll go to the vets with you!'"

"Shhh!" said Bertie. "Not so loud!"

"Don't be daft, Bertie," said Gran. "He's a dog! He can't understand a word we're saying!"

The dog lead suddenly yanked her backwards and they both turned around. Whiffer had stopped and was lying down on the pavement.

"See?" said Bertie. "You said the word. Now we'll never get him there."

He clapped his hands. "Come on, Whiffer! Let's go!"

But Whiffer wouldn't budge. Bertie pleaded with him. He spoke in his dog-training voice. He tried to drag Whiffer along by his lead but Whiffer dug in his heels and refused to budge.

"Now what?" sighed Gran.

Bertie tried to think. If they didn't get Whiffer to the vets there'd be no five pound reward.

"Maggots!" he said suddenly.

"Maggots?" said Gran. "The poor dog's got fleas already! Bertie, this isn't one of your harebrained ideas, is it?"

"No," said Bertie. "Trust me, Gran, this will work. When Dad goes fishing he uses maggots. The fish come after them. So what we need is something that Whiffer will come after!"

Gran looked at him. "Why do I get the feeling I'm going to regret this?"

"You won't," said Bertie. "I promise. Just lend me your key."

CHAPTER 3

Ten minutes later Bertie was back. Gran stared. He was wearing his helmet and roller blades, and pulling a bag that trundled along on two wheels.

"That's my shopping bag!" said Gran.

"I know," said Bertie, beaming. "It's perfect! And look what I found in the fridge!"

Dirty Bertie

He unzipped the bag to reveal a string of sausages. "And that's my supper!" said Gran. "What are you up to?"

"It's simple," explained Bertie. "I skate along with the sausages in the bag. As soon as Whiffer sees them he'll start chasing me. He loves sausages!"

"And what am I doing while you're zooming off with my supper?" asked Gran.

"You hold on to Whiffer's lead," said Bertie. "Don't let him catch the sausages or it won't work."

Gran shook her head. "I must be barmy to listen to you."

Bertie's plan worked perfectly — at least to begin with. Bertie whizzed off on his

Dirty Bertie

roller blades with the sausages trailing
from the shopping bag. As soon as Whiffer
spotted them he barked and sprang to
his feet. Then he was off, dragging Gran
behind him at turbo speed.

"Hang on, Gran!" Bertie called over his
shoulder.

"I am hanging on!" puffed Gran. "Can't
you tell him to slow down?"

Bertie skated through the precinct,
weaving in and out of shoppers. Whiffer
bounded along behind, tugging at his
lead and barking excitedly. People
stopped to stare at the old lady chasing
a dog who was chasing a string of
sausages.

Everything might have been all right if
Whiffer hadn't barked so loudly. But
Whiffer always barked when he was

excited and he was excited now. As they
came tearing down Riddle Road, the
Alsatian at Number 12 heard Whiffer
barking. Seeing some escaping sausages,
he eagerly joined the chase. Further
down the road they met the terrier at
47 and the scruffy mongrel at 72. Both
of them were fond of sausages and even
fonder of a good chase.

Dirty Bertie

"Help!" cried Gran. "Bertie stop! I'm being attacked!"

Bertie looked behind him. Gran had a pack of dogs snapping at her heels. She was red in the face and skidding along like a tomato on water-skis. Whiffer was gaining on the sausages. Bertie skated faster. He could see the vets at the end of the road.

"Hang on Gran, we're almost there!" he yelled.

Dirty Bertie

Turning sharp left, he whizzed into the drive, up a ramp and through the open door. The receptionist met him in the hall with a pile of files in her arms. Her mouth dropped open.

"I CAN'T STOP!" warned Bertie. He ploughed straight into her, scattering papers everywhere. The shopping bag did a somersault over Bertie's head and the sausages came flying out. A warm, wet tongue licked his face as Whiffer bounded on top of him.

Gran arrived soon after, panting heavily. "Well that worked a treat," she said.

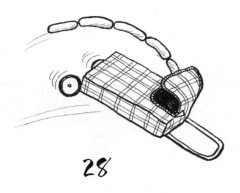

CHAPTER 4

"Have they gone?" asked Bertie.

Gran glanced out of the window. "No, I'm afraid not."

They were sitting in Mr Cage's waiting room. Outside the Alsatian and his friends kept watch by the door. They had been thrown out once but they weren't giving up that easily.

29

Dirty Bertie

The receptionist seemed to think it was all Bertie's fault. She said he had no business bringing every dog in the neighbourhood. Bertie tried to explain they weren't his dogs but the receptionist went on telling him off. Then Gran got cross too, and said if she didn't get a glass of water soon they'd have to call an ambulance.

At least I got Whiffer to the vets, thought Bertie. Whiffer was sitting at his feet, happily slobbering over the sausages. It seemed to have escaped his notice that he was in a vet's waiting room. Bertie glanced round the room at the other pets. There was a parrot, a hamster, a snake curled up in a box, and a poodle that looked like a powder puff on legs.

Scratch! Scratch! Scratch! Whiffer's back leg was itching again.

The owner of the poodle looked down her nose at Bertie. "What's wrong with your dog?"

"Oh he's fine really," said Bertie. "Just a few fleas."

"Fleas? I hope you're joking?"

"No," said Bertie, "I can show you if you like." He reached into his pocket. But the woman got up from her chair and quickly backed away. She called to her poodle.

"Fifi! Fifi, darling! Get away from that filthy fleabag."

"He's not a filthy fleabag!" said Bertie.
"He had a bath last month."

The woman picked up her poodle and
sat down on the other side of the room.
Bertie and Gran were left sitting by
themselves. Gran was chuckling to
herself. Bertie hoped that Whiffer had
managed to pass a few of his fleas to Fifi.

Just then the door to the street
opened and a woman entered, carrying
a fat ginger cat. Whiffer looked up and
growled. Bertie noticed the door had
been left open.

"'Scuse me!" he said. "You'd better shut
that! There's some…"

But the warning came too late. The
Alsatian and his friends had seen their
chance. In a few seconds the waiting
room was full of barking, yapping,

growling dogs. The Alsatian chased the
ginger cat round a table. Whiffer and the
terrier snarled and fought over the string
of sausages. And the parrot flew over
their heads squawking, "Give us a kiss!
Give us a kiss!"

"What's the plan now?" shouted Gran in Bertie's ear.

"I'm working on it!" replied Bertie. He tried to catch Whiffer as he ran past.

Hearing the bedlam, Mr Cage came running in and soon wished he hadn't. The cat sprang off the table and sunk its claws into his leg. Whiffer, seeing his old enemy, jumped up and knocked him to the floor. The cat and the barking dogs then used the vet as a roundabout as they chased each other in circles. Finally they escaped out the door with Whiffer leading the way.

There was a long silence as Mr Cage sat up and stared at the wreckage of his waiting room. Bertie bent over him.

"Um, I was wondering," he asked. "Do you know anything about fleas?"

Dirty Bertie

Dirty Bertie

Dad was still working at the computer when Bertie got home.

"How did it go?" he asked, not looking up.

"Oh," replied Bertie. "It was okay, but—"

"You did get Whiffer to the vets?" Dad interrupted.

"Oh yes, I got him there."

"And you told Mr Cage about the fleas?"

"Yes I told him, but the thing was—"

Dad held up a hand to cut him off. "Tell me later, Bertie, I've just got to finish this." He pulled out a five-pound note from his wallet. "Thanks. And don't mention it to Mum, eh? It can be our secret."

Dirty Bertie

Bertie took the five-pound note and left. He'd tried to explain but that was the trouble with grown-ups, they never had time to listen. Anyway he had a feeling Mum and Dad would find out the truth soon enough. Perhaps when Mr Cage phoned about the damage. Or when they noticed that Whiffer was still crawling with fleas. So it was probably best to spend the money while he had the chance.

Bertie took the matchbox from his pocket and slid it open a fraction.

"Now," he said, peering inside. "Where could we buy a trapeze?"

DARE!

CHAPTER 1

Bertie's class had a new teacher. Mr
Weakly was young, pale and very
nervous, with round glasses that made
him look like a startled owl. He was
standing in for Miss Boot while she
was off sick. Bertie thought she probably
had a sore throat from all that shouting
she did.

Dirty Bertie

He sat at the back of the class
whispering with Darren. They were
playing the Dare Game. They wouldn't
have risked anything so dangerous if Miss
Boot had been around. Miss Boot could
see you even when her back was
turned. But Mr Weakly didn't shout or
go purple in the face like Miss Boot; he
hardly seemed to get cross at all. Darren
had already dared Bertie to burp loudly
and Bertie had dared Darren to "drop
dead" on the floor. Mr Weakly
had merely looked up from his
book and asked
them not to be silly.

Dirty Bertie

"So?" said Bertie. "What's the dare?"

"I'm thinking," said Darren. Darren never won the Dare Game because Bertie was daring enough to do anything. Darren had once dared him to shout "Pants!" in assembly and Bertie had yelled it at the top of his voice. But this time he was going to think of something much harder, something that even Bertie wouldn't dare to do. A smile slowly spread across his face. He had it.

"Okay," he said. "I dare you to lock Mr Weakly in the store room."

Bertie gaped at him. "What?"

"That's the dare," said Darren. "I did mine, now it's your turn. Unless you're chickening out."

"Who says I'm chickening out?" said Bertie.

Dirty Bertie

Bertie glanced over at the store room. It was little more than a tiny cupboard which Miss Boot kept locked at all times. Bertie had been in there once to get some computer paper. It was stuffy and the light didn't work. He wondered if Mr Weakly was scared of the dark... Still, a dare was a dare and he wasn't about to back down.

"All right," he said. "I'll do it."

Bertie's chance came a few minutes later. Mr Weakly took off his reading glasses and asked them to copy some questions into their workbooks. Bertie raised his hand.

"Yes? What is it?" asked Mr Weakly.

"I've run out of space in my workbook, sir," said Bertie.

Dirty Bertie

"Oh," said Mr Weakly. "Um, what do you normally do?"

"Miss Boot keeps new workbooks in the store room," said Bertie, pointing at the door. "The key's in the drawer."

"Thank you, um…" said Mr Weakly, forgetting Bertie's name. "The rest of you carry on with your work."

Mr Weakly found the key and unlocked the store room door. He disappeared inside, leaving the door open and the key in the lock. Bertie could hear him rummaging on the shelves, looking for the workbooks.

"Go on!" whispered Darren. "Before he comes out!"

Bertie slid out of his seat and crept towards the door. One or two of the class looked up from their work.

Dirty Bertie

Bertie reached out a hand.

"SLAM!"
The door swung shut.
"CLICK!"
The key turned in the lock.
"OH!"
cried Mr Weakly from inside.
"What's happening?"

Bertie pocketed the key and turned to Darren in triumph. The class were all staring at him open-mouthed.

"You've locked him in!" said Darren.

"I know," grinned Bertie. "That was the dare."

"Yeah, but I didn't think you'd actually do it. What are you going to do now?" asked Darren.

Bertie's grin faded — he hadn't really thought that far ahead. He supposed Mr Weakly might be a bit cross. More than a bit in fact. If he'd locked Miss Boot in the store room she would have snorted like a mad bull.

"You're for it," said Donna.

"He's going to kill you," said Know-All Nick.

"No he isn't," said Bertie. "How does he know it was me?"

CHAPTER 2

THUMP! THUMP! Mr Weakly was
knocking on the door.

"Children!" he pleaded. "Really, this isn't
funny. I'm going to count to three." He
counted to three. "One ... two ...
three." Nothing happened.

Eugene looked anxious. "We can't just
leave him there," he said.

Dirty Bertie

"You let him out then," said Darren.
"I'm not getting into trouble."

"Why me?" said Eugene. "I didn't lock
him in, Bertie did."

They all turned to look at Bertie who
had crossed to Mr Weakly's desk.

He had always wondered what it
would be like to sit in the
teacher's chair. He picked
up Mr Weakly's reading
glasses and put them on. He
added Mr Weakly's jacket.

Dirty Bertie

"Too much chatter!" he said, sternly.
"Get on with your work!"

"You look like a teacher," giggled
Donna.

"I am a teacher," said Bertie. "I'm a
very strict teacher and you'll all be
staying in at playtime if you don't behave!"

The class laughed. Bertie sounded like
Miss Boot in a bad mood.

Dirty Bertie

He peered at them over his glasses. "Who made that pong?" he demanded. "Nick, was that you?"

The class howled with laughter. Know-All Nick turned scarlet.

"You wait. You're in so much trouble," he said. "When Miss Skinner finds out, she'll go up the wall."

Dirty Bertie

Bertie hadn't thought of Miss Skinner.
The head teacher had a nasty habit of
looking in on a class unexpectedly. If Miss
Skinner found out he'd locked Mr Weakly
in the store room there'd be trouble.
The thumps were getting louder. Bertie
eyed the door. Maybe he should unlock
it? If he moved fast he could be back in
his seat before Mr Weakly got free. He
felt in his pocket. He plunged his hand in
deeper. A look of horror crossed his
face.

"It's gone!" he said. "I've lost the key!"

"Ha ha!" said Darren. "Come on
Bertie, stop messing around."

"I'm not messing around! I put it in my
pocket just now."

Bertie turned out his pocket and saw
the small hole in the lining.

Dirty Bertie

The key must have slipped through and fallen out. What if he couldn't find it? What if Mr Weakly was locked in the store room *for ever?*

"Don't just stand there!" he cried. "Help me look!"

Bertie, Darren and Donna got down on their hands and knees to search the floor.

Know-All Nick leaned back in his chair, smiling. "I told you," he jeered. "You are in *so* much trouble, Bertie."

Eugene had been keeping watch at the window. "Hurry up!" he warned. "Someone's coming!"

"What?" said Bertie.

Dirty Bertie

The class crowded at the window to look. A woman with wild red hair was striding purposefully across the courtyard towards them.

"Oh her," said Know-all Nick. "She's the school inspector. Miss Skinner said she was coming today."

"Inspector?" said Bertie, horrified. "What's she inspecting?"

"Our school. Weren't you listening in assembly? I expect she wants to inspect Mr Weakly."

Dirty Bertie

They all looked at the store room door. Mr Weakly was rattling the handle.

"We've got to get him out!" said Bertie, starting to panic.

"We?" said Know-All Nick. "You locked him in there, *you* get him out."

"But I can't find the key!" moaned Bertie.

"Do something!" cried Eugene. "She's coming up the stairs."

"Wait, I've got an idea," said Donna. "Bertie can pretend he's our teacher."

"What?" said Bertie.

"Pretend to be Mr Weakly. You're wearing his jacket and glasses. Just say you're him."

"Are you crazy?" said Bertie. "She'll know I'm not him!"

"No she won't, she's probably never

met him. All you have to do is sit at a desk and act like a teacher. You can do it!"

"Yeah," said Darren. "I dare you!"

Bertie shot Darren a look. But maybe Donna was right. He was always doing impressions of Miss Boot, so why couldn't he be Mr Weakly? In any case he didn't have a better idea. He sat down at the teacher's desk. The class were all out of their seats, milling around like lost sheep.

"Well SIT DOWN!" cried Bertie. "Look as if you're working!"

Everyone ran to their desks and sat down. Even Know-All Nick did as he was told. Bertie was amazed at his own power. He gave an order and everyone obeyed him. So this was what it was like to be a teacher!

CHAPTER 3

Miss Barker knocked on the classroom door and entered. She had heard scuffling as she approached but now the class all seemed to be working quietly. A scruffy boy sat at the teacher's desk in a jacket that was far too big for him.

"Good morning. My name is Miss Barker," she said. "Where is your teacher?"

"Yes, good morning," replied Bertie. "I am the teacher."

"Don't be ridiculous!" snapped Miss Barker. "Where is Mr Weakly?"

"Yes, Mr Weakly. That's my name," nodded Bertie, his glasses sliding down his nose. He pushed them back up again.

Miss Barker peered down at the boy. Teachers seemed to be getting younger and younger these days, but this was absurd. This one hardly looked any older than the rest of the class. When she'd first entered the room she could have sworn he had a finger up his nose.

"How old are you?" she demanded.

"Seven ... seventeen," said Bertie, correcting himself quickly.

"Seventeen? That's far too young to be a teacher!"

Dirty Bertie

"Yes," said Bertie. "It is for a normal teacher but it's 'cos I'm more cleverer than normal."

"More cleverer?" repeated Miss Barker.

"Yes," said Bertie. "I used to get ten out of tens at school all the time. So in the end they said I just ought to get on and start teaching."

Miss Barker was about to reply but she was interrupted by a strange knocking sound.

"What's that noise?" she said.

"What noise?" asked Bertie.

"That banging noise."

"Oh that," said Bertie. "That's just Miss Todd, teaching next door. She gets a bit cross sometimes and she starts banging on the walls and things."

"Banging on the walls? Good heavens!" said Miss Barker.

She made a note in her black file and turned back to Bertie. "Well," she said, "if you really are Mr Weakly you better get on with the lesson."

"What?" said Bertie.

"The lesson. The lesson you're teaching."

"Oh yes, that," said Bertie. He gulped and pushed his glasses back up his nose. Miss Barker's face had gone all blurry. She seemed to be waiting for him to start. But what could he teach? He knew a lot about fleas – maybe he should draw some fleas on the board?

Dirty Bertie

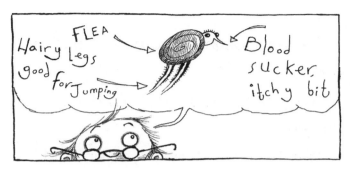

The banging from the store room started up again. He had to do something to drown out the noise.

"Maths!" he said, practically shouting. "We were just going to do a few sums." The class stared at him blankly, all except Darren who was pulling faces at him from the back row.

"Darren!" said Bertie.

"Yes?"

"Stand up," said Bertie. Darren stood up.

"What is two plus two?" asked Bertie.

Darren thought a moment. "Four," he said.

"Very good, sit down," said Bertie. "Eugene."

"Yes, Bertie ... I mean yes, sir," said Eugene, standing up.

"What are three twos, Eugene?"

"Six!" squeaked Eugene.

"Very good," said Bertie. "Nick."

Know-All Nick got to his feet. "Miss Barker—" he began, but Bertie cut him off.

"Pay attention, Nick. What is 2,740 times 7 million?"

Know-All Nick's mouth dropped open.

"Come on, come on," said Bertie, enjoying himself. "I haven't got all day!"

"I ... I ... don't know," stammered Know-All Nick.

Dirty Bertie

Bertie peered over his glasses. "Tut tut, Nick! Extra homework for you tonight."

CHAPTER 4

THUMP! THUMP! THUMP! The banging from the store room was deafening.

"Help!" cried Mr Weakly. "Can anyone hear me?"

Miss Barker stood up. "There's someone behind that door!" she said.

"No um ah … I don't think so," mumbled Bertie.

Dirty Bertie

"Let me out! PLEASE!" begged Mr Weakly.

"There is someone in there," said Miss Barker. "I can hear them shouting!"

Bertie's heart sank. Miss Barker hurried over to the store room and spoke through the door.

"Hello?"

"Hello!" replied Mr Weakly. "Thank heavens! Who's that?"

"This is Miss Barker – the school inspector."

"Oh dear!" said Mr Weakly in a faint voice.

"What are you doing in there?"

"I'm locked in!" said Mr Weakly. "I came in to get a book and the door shut and now I'm locked in."

"Wait there!" said the inspector. "I'm going to fetch a teacher."

"I *am* a teacher," said Mr Weakly. "I'm Mr Weakly."

Miss Barker looked puzzled. "But I thought … Mr Weakly is right here…"

She turned back to the teacher's desk. But there was no sign of the scruffy boy she had been talking to – only a pair of glasses and a crumpled jacket that lay on his chair. Bertie had seized his chance to escape… He'd had enough of teaching for today. As he slid into his place he felt something sharp in his pocket. He pulled it out and stared at the silver key in surprise.

"Look!" he whispered to Darren. "It was in my other pocket all the time!"

Dirty Bertie

Know-All Nick had turned round in his seat. He raised his hand in the air.

"Miss Barker! Miss Barker!" he said. "Bertie's got something to show you!"

Dirty Bertie

The next day Miss Boot was back.

"Let's begin with Art," she said, with a gleam in her eye. "We'll need brushes and powder paints. Bertie, perhaps you'd like to fetch them from the store room?"

Bertie turned pale. He suddenly didn't feel well. "ME?" he said.

Dirty Bertie

FIRE!

CHAPTER 1

BOOF! Bertie landed two-footed in the big pile of leaves, scattering them everywhere.

"My go!" said Darren.

"HEY, YOU TWO! OFF THERE!" roared an angry voice. A bald, red-faced man was striding across the playground towards them.

Dirty Bertie

"Uh-oh," said Darren. It was Mr Grouch, the school caretaker.

"What do you think you're doing?" demanded Mr Grouch.

"Um, jumping in leaves," said Bertie.

"Do you know how long it took me to sweep those up?" shouted Mr Grouch, waving his broom.

Bertie picked up a leaf and put it back on the pile. "Sorry Mr Grouch, we were only playing."

"Well DON'T play! Not where I'm working."

"But this is a playground."

Mr Grouch narrowed his eyes. "Are you trying to be funny?"

"No, Mr Grouch," replied Bertie.

"Then don't answer back. And keep out of my way!"

Dirty Bertie

Mr Grouch glared after Bertie and Darren as they trudged off. Mr Grouch didn't like children and he didn't like mess. Most of all he didn't like Bertie. It was Bertie who left muddy footprints all over Mr Grouch's newly washed floors. It was Bertie who drew faces on Mr Grouch's spotless windows.

Dirty Bertie

And Mr Grouch was sure it was
Bertie who had flooded the boys' toilets
by trying to flush away an entire toilet
roll. In Mr
Grouch's view,
Bertie was a
menace. In
Bertie's view,
Mr Grouch was a
vampire with a broom.

"What shall we do now?"
asked Darren, as they watched the
caretaker sweep the leaves back into a
neat pile. Bertie wasn't listening. He was
staring at something coming along the
road. A shiny red fire engine was slowing
down and signalling left. Bertie watched
with growing excitement as it turned in
through the school gates.

Dirty Bertie

The fire engine halted in the car park in front of the school and a woman in a smart blue uniform climbed out. Bertie and Darren hurried over.

"What's happening? Is the school on fire?" asked Bertie, hopefully.

"I'm afraid not," laughed the woman. "I'm Val, what's your name?"

"Bertie. Are you a fireman?"

"Well I'm a fire fighter. We're here on

Dirty Bertie

a visit. Didn't Miss Skinner tell you we were coming?"

Mr Grouch came storming over with a face like thunder. He pointed at the fire engine. "You can't leave that there! It's in my way."

Val smiled. "Sorry, Miss Skinner said to park it there."

"Did she now? We'll see about that!" said Mr Grouch, and he stormed off muttering to himself.

"Oh, dear," said Val, pulling a face. "Am I in trouble?"

"That's nothing," said Bertie. "You should try jumping in a pile of leaves."

CHAPTER 2

Bertie could hardly believe it — a real fire
crew! His school hardly ever got visitors.
The last one they had was the nurse
who checked them for head lice.
The fire crew stayed all morning and
spoke to the whole school. Bertie
learned how to dial 999 and what to do
in case of a fire.

Dirty Bertie

Outside Bertie and his friends staggered around wearing helmets on their heads. They sat in the red engine and turned on the flashing blue light. Finally they helped the fire crew unroll a hose that stretched all the way across the playground.

"Can we turn it on?" asked Bertie.

"Sorry, Bertie, not allowed," said Val. "Only if there's a real fire."

Bertie wished he could help put out a real fire. He imagined the school crackling with flames and all the teachers at the windows crying for help. He would climb up the huge long ladder and carry them down one by one. (Miss Boot could wait till last. Come to think of it, Miss Boot could climb down by herself.)

Dirty Bertie

Dirty Bertie

At lunchtime, Bertie and his friends
gazed across at the fire engine longingly.
"I wish we could play on it," sighed
Bertie.

"Miss Boot said we're not allowed,"
said Eugene.

"Well I think it's cruelty," said Bertie.
"Leaving a fire engine right next to a
playground and then telling us we're not
allowed to play on it. It's cruelty to
children."

Know-All Nick had sidled up to them
unnoticed. "I bet none of you have
ridden in a fire engine," he said. "I have!"

"When?" said Bertie.

"Hundreds of times," said Know-All
Nick. "My uncle's a fireman and he lets

me go in it whenever I like."

"I bet he doesn't," said Bertie. "How come we've never seen you?"

Know-All Nick shrugged. "Next time I'll ask him to drive right past your house, Bertie."

Bertie snorted. Know-All Nick was always making things up. Once he told them that he'd seen the Queen queuing at the bus stop. Bertie didn't believe that and he didn't believe Nick's uncle drove a fire engine. He probably drove a milk van.

"Anyway," said Bertie. "We don't want to go in your smelly old fire engine. We've got our own." He gripped an imaginary steering wheel and flicked an imaginary switch in front of him. "Come on!" he said.

Dirty Bertie

"WOO! WOO! WOO!" went Bertie's siren as he drove off with Darren, Donna and Eugene hanging on behind him. Nick scowled, watching them go.

They drove the fire engine four times round the playground, stopping to put out several fires on the way. When they'd had enough they flopped down on the grass to rest.

"Oh no," groaned Darren. "He's back." Know-All Nick was running towards them, waving his arms excitedly.

"Quick!" he panted. "The school's on fire!"

"Yeah, very funny," said Bertie.

"I'm not joking," said Know-All Nick. "Look over there if you don't believe me!" He pointed to the far corner of the school. They all looked. Clouds of grey smoke rose into the sky above the roof of the hall.

"WOW!" said Bertie, getting to his feet. "It *is* on fire!"

Eugene stared open-mouthed. "What are we going to do?"

"Get the fire brigade!" said Donna. "I'll run to the staff room!"

"No!" said Know-All Nick, blocking her way. "They're not in there. I looked!"

"Then where are they?"

"I don't know!" said Nick. "Maybe they went out for sandwiches. But if we don't do something it'll be too late."

Dirty Bertie

Bertie suddenly saw things clearly. For once, Nick was right. There was no time to search for the fire crew. The school was burning down and only he – Fire Fighter Bertie – could save it. Soon the flames would spread and in minutes the whole school would be ablaze. Trapped inside, the teachers would be burned to a frazzle. It was up to him.

"Come on!" he said.

"Where are we going?" said Darren.

"To put out the fire, of course!"

"But isn't that dangerous?" worried Eugene. "Shouldn't we fetch Miss Boot?"

"Miss Boot's no use," said Bertie. "This is a job for professionals."

Bertie reached the fire engine first. The clouds of smoke were billowing higher. He took command, shouting orders.

Dirty Bertie

"Grab the hose! Now start pulling! Eugene, you get ready to turn it on."

"Okay!" nodded Eugene.

The orange hose began to unwind as Bertie, Darren and Donna dragged it towards the clouds of smoke. Other children came running to see what the noise was about. Eugene wished he had time to go to the toilet. Know-All Nick sat under a tree, watching them with a knowing smile.

At last they dragged the hose round the corner of the school. The smoke wasn't coming from the hall but from the yard behind it. Clouds of smoke stung Bertie's eyes, half blinding him.

"Now, Eugene!" he shouted. "Turn it on!"

Dirty Bertie

The hose gurgled, coughed and sprang into life. A jet of water shot out with a tremendous whoosh. The hose wriggled like a snake, spraying water in every direction.

"Hold it still!" urged Bertie.

"We're trying!" said Donna. At last Bertie wrestled it under control and pointed it at the fire. With a hiss, the flames died down and fizzled out.

Dirty Bertie

"We did it!" cried Bertie. "We saved the school." But as the smoke cleared he caught sight of Mr Grouch who had been knocked right off his feet by the first blast from the hose.

"Turn it off!" he gurgled.

Bertie stared in horror. His fire crew dropped the hose and ran. The school wasn't on fire at all. The only "fire" was Mr Grouch's bonfire, which was now a pile of damp, smoking leaves.

Dirty Bertie

Mr Grouch sat in a puddle with water dripping from his soggy overalls.

"You wait, you little pest!" he growled. "You just wait!"

Bertie decided it was better not to wait. He turned and ran, with the angry caretaker squelching after him. He could hear Know-All Nick's shrill voice calling after him.

"Run Bertie, run! YOUR PANTS ARE ON FIRE!"

CHAPTER 3

It was all Know-All Nick's fault, thought
Bertie, as he swept up the soggy leaves.
Nick had tricked him just to get him in
trouble. But how was he to know the
school wasn't on fire? You'd think
teachers would be grateful when you
tried to save their lives. You'd think they'd
want to thank you.

Dirty Bertie

But no – the way Miss Boot talked, anyone would think he'd tried to drown Mr Grouch on purpose! Well next time the school could just burn down.

"Can't I stop now?" he asked. "It's almost home time."

Mr Grouch looked at his watch. "Go on then. But don't think you're getting off lightly. Your parents will be hearing about this."

Bertie trudged home gloomily. Turning into Church Lane, he saw Pamela from his class. She was standing under a tree, gazing up at a white kitten clinging to one of the branches. It mewed pitifully.

"Poor thing!" said Pamela. "I've been calling her for ages. I think she's scared."

Dirty Bertie

"Oh," said Bertie. "D'you want me to get her down for you?"

He eyed the kitten sternly and spoke to it in his dog-training voice.

"Here girl! Down girl!" The kitten stared back at him without moving.

"I'll have to climb up," said Bertie.

Pamela looked up. "It's very high."

"Oh that's not high to me," said Bertie. "I've climbed hundreds of trees higher than that."

He took off his bag and jacket and caught hold of the lowest branch.

Luckily the tree was the kind that was made for climbing. Bertie wished there were more people to see his daring rescue.

89

Dirty Bertie

As he climbed higher he pictured the kitten clinging gratefully to his chest. He could see her sitting on the end of a long branch. Bertie began to inch his way along, lying flat on his stomach.

"Have you got her?" called Pamela.

"Almost!" He reached out a hand. "Here puss! Here!"

The kitten got to its feet. But instead of going to Bertie, it yawned lazily and jumped down to the branch below.

In a few swift leaps and bounds it had reached the ground. Pamela scooped it up in her arms joyfully.

Dirty Bertie

"It's okay, Bertie! I've got her!"
she called. "She's all
right!"
Looking down, Bertie
suddenly felt *he* wasn't
all right. The ground
seemed a long way below —
much further than he thought.
In fact he wasn't sure how he
was going to get down. His
hands were sweating and he'd
started to feel dizzy. He
wrapped himself round the
branch, not daring to move.
Pamela's voice floated up to him.

"Bertie? What are you doing?
You can come down now!"

"Um … I think you'd better
call for help," said Bertie.

CHAPTER 4

An hour later Bertie sat in the passenger seat of the fire engine.

"What road did you say?" asked Val.

"Digby Drive," said Bertie.

Val nodded. "I hope you're not planning to make a habit of this," she smiled, "because next time you'll be walking home!"

Dirty Bertie

Bertie's rescue from the tree had caused quite a stir. A small crowd had gathered to watch when the fire engine arrived. A ladder was extended to Bertie with Val on top to help him down. When they were safe on the ground, everyone clapped and Bertie took a bow.

But the best part of all was that he got to ride home in the fire engine.

He looked out of the window. They were passing Cecil Road. Suddenly Bertie had a brilliant idea.

"Um, could we just turn down here?" he pointed. "It's sort of on the way, and there's someone I wanted to see."

Dirty Bertie

Know-All Nick was in the lounge,
watching his favourite cartoon on TV.
WOOO! WOOO! WOOO! A
deafening noise outside made him
jump. He hurried over to the open
window and looked out. He blinked.
Was he dreaming?

A red fire engine was driving very
slowly past his house with its lights
flashing and its siren blaring. And sitting
in the front seat, wearing a helmet and
waving to him was Dirty Bertie. The
siren stopped.

"Hi, Nick!" called Bertie. "Somebody
called 999. They said to come to your
house right away."

"My house?" said Nick. "Why?"

Dirty Bertie

"BECAUSE YOUR PANTS ARE ON FIRE!" shouted Bertie.